Crossing Bok Chitto

A Choctaw Tale of Friendship & Freedom

by **TIM TINGLE**

illustrated by

JEANNE ROREX BRIDGES

THERE IS A RIVER CALLED BOK CHITTO that cuts through Mississippi. In the days before the War Between the States, in the days before the Trail of Tears, Bok Chitto was a boundary. On one side of the river lived the Choctaws, a nation of Indian people. On the other side lived the plantation owners and their slaves. If a slave escaped and made his way across Bok Chitto, the slave was free. The slave owner could not follow. That was the law.

One Sunday morning during this time, a Choctaw momma woke her daughter up.

"Martha Tom, the sun has been up for two hours. Get up and put your dress on, you lazy little girl! I have a wedding to cook for today. Take this basket and fill it with blackberries. Now hurry back."

When Martha Tom couldn't find blackberries on the Choctaw side of the river, she did something she'd been told never to do—she went crossing Bok Chitto. The only way to cross Bok Chitto in those days was a stone path just beneath the surface of the river. Only the Choctaws knew it was there, for the Choctaws had built it. When the river flooded, they built the stones up. When the river sank in times of drought, they built the stones down, always just beneath the muddy surface of the water.

Martha Tom found a patch of blackberries on the slave side of the river. She filled her basket, then looked to the sky for the sun to lead her home. But it was cloudy and she was lost. Martha Tom thought she was approaching the river, but instead she was walking still deeper into the woods.

She came upon a stump covered with grape vines. Before her lay a clearing filled with logs, rolled out as if they were benches. Martha Tom saw someone coming and dove into the vines. A skinny black man with a cane stepped out of the trees. While Martha Tom watched, he climbed onto the stump and called out, "We are bound for the Promised Land!"

What happened next would change Martha Tom's life forever.
Though she saw no one, a hundred voices came in reply, like spirit
voices, whispering, "We are bound for the Promised Land!"

The old man called out again, "We are bound for the Promised Land!"

Once again she heard the voices, human voices this time, closer and
closer they came, calling, "We are bound for the Promised Land!" The
old man bowed his head and said, "Oh, who will come and go with me?"

A hundred slaves replied, stepping from behind the trees and rising
up from the bushes where they were hiding.

"We will come and go with you.

We are bound for the Promised Land!"

It was the calling together of the forbidden slave church, deep in those Mississippi woods. The old man began to preach and the people began to sing. Martha Tom had never heard music like this before, but it touched her deeply.

Then something else touched her—on the shoulder. She looked up to see the biggest man she had ever seen, his chest so big it was about to pop his buttons off his shirt!

"You're lost, little girl?" he said in a deep voice that seemed to smile. "You're Choctaw, from across Bok Chitto?"

Martha Tom nodded.

"What is your name, little girl?"

"Martha Tom."

"Well, Martha Tom, I'll get my son to take you back to the river. You can find your way home from there. Little Mo!" he called.

A boy appeared. "Little Mo, this girl is lost. She is Choctaw from across Bok Chitto. Take her to the riverbank and she can get home from there."

"Daddy, I better not do that," Little Mo said. "The men from the plantation house told us if the children are seen playing near the river, our whole family will get in trouble."

His father knelt down to Little Mo and said, "Son, son, it's about time you learned. There is a way to move amongst them where they won't even notice you. It's like you're invisible. You move not too fast, not too slow, eyes to the ground, away you go! Now give it a try and get this little girl home!"

Well, it sounded like a fun game to play, so Little Mo took Martha Tom by the hand and off they went, just as Little Mo's daddy had taught him, not too fast, not too slow, eyes to the ground, away you go!

They skirted the plantation house and walked right in front
of the porch, where the owners were doing their sipping and
sighing that Sunday morning. But no one paid them any mind.
"We must be invisible," thought Little Mo.

They soon arrived at the river and it was Martha Tom's turn to lead. She took Little Mo to the path, but he couldn't see the stones beneath the muddy water.

"This will be a fun game to play," she thought. She walked five paces back to get a good running start, then leapt to the river! Little Mo reached out to grab her dress as she flew by, to keep her from drowning.

When Martha Tom landed in the river, she stood up!
"Little girl, what kind of witch are you?" Little Mo cried.
Martha Tom laughed, "I'm not any kind of witch. You
can do it, too! Come on!"
She took Little Mo by the hand and together the two
of them went crossing Bok Chitto to the Choctaw side.

Even before they stepped from the stones to the earth, Little Mo heard the sound of chanting. He thought it must be the heartbeat of the earth itself. It was the old men calling the Choctaws to the wedding ceremony.

Martha Tom and Little Mo looked down the street of log homes as Choctaw women stepped out of every doorway. Their white cotton dresses skimmed the ground and their shiny black hair fell well below their waists. The women formed a line and began a stomp dance to the beat of the chanting, gliding to a clearing at the end of town.

When they reached the clearing, they formed two circles, the women and the men, and the wedding ceremony began. The old men began to sing the old wedding song. It is still sung today in Mississippi and Oklahoma, just as they sang it then.

> "Way, hey ya hey ya   Way, hey ya hey ya
> You a hey you ay   You a hey you ay
> A hey ya a hey ya!   A hey ya a hey ya!"

Little Mo had never heard music like this before, but it touched him deeply.

Then something else touched them both, on the shoulder.
It was Martha Tom's mother!

"Little girl, little girl, you have been crossing Bok Chitto!
Now I'm not mad at him, but you take him to the river and
come right back. And give me those blackberries! You are
in for it now!"

Martha Tom knew her mother could cackle like a mad
crow on the outside, while inside she would coo like a dove
with love for her daughter. She took Little Mo to the river
and showed him how to cross on his own. And so began
a friendship that would last for years.

Every Sunday morning Martha Tom would cross Bok Chitto on her way to church. She sat with Little Mo's family now. She listened to the preaching and she sang the songs in English. Then every evening she would sing them in Choctaw as she went crossing Bok Chitto on her way home.

Then one day trouble came. It always does, in stories or in life, trouble comes. There was a slave sale and twenty slaves were sold. They were to leave for New Orleans the very next day before sunrise. The men from the slave households were called together to listen to the names being read. Little Mo's mother was on that list.

As he walked home, Little Mo's father wondered how to tell his family what had happened. He decided to let them have their last meal in peace.

When the children stood to clear the table, he motioned for them to be seated. Feeling his knees grow weak, he said, "Your mother has been sold."

"Nooo!" she cried. The tears seemed to squirt down her cheeks. The children looked at their parents and began to cry. They had never seen their mother and father like this.

"This is our last evening together!" he said. "Stop your crying. I want every one of you to find something small and precious, something to give your mother to remember you by, something she can hide, something they can't take away. Now, get up and help your mother pack. You will not see her again."

No one moved.

Then Little Mo pulled his father's sleeve and said, "Daddy, there is a way we can stay together. We can go crossing Bok Chitto. Martha Tom told me how."

"Son, they'll have the dogs guarding the river tonight, to prevent a crossing."

"Daddy, we can go just like you taught me—not too fast, not too slow, eyes to the ground, away you go! We'll be invisible. Daddy, we have to give it a try."

For the first time that day, hope filled the father's heart. "You are right, son. We have to give it a try."

He grabbed seven burlap bags and gave one to each member of his family, saying, "Pack quickly, pack light, and pack for running. We may have to." They did pack quickly, they packed light, but they were not quick enough.

The men in the plantation house saw them working late. They called for the guards with the dogs and the lanterns and the guns, and they surrounded that little house.

When Little Mo's daddy stood with his family around him, he looked out the back door and said, "We could go out that way. It would be dark and maybe safer. But this night's journey is not about darkness and safety. It is about faith. It is about freedom. We will go out the front door."

And so they did, out the front door, down the front steps, walking just as Little Mo had reminded them—not too fast, not too slow, eyes to the ground, away you go!

Then something remarkable happened. This family became invisible! They walked into the circle of lanterns, but the light shone right through them. They walked so close to the dogs they could have stroked the dogs' fur, but even the dogs did not know they were there. They were invisible.

Soon they stood on the banks of Bok Chitto. Little Mo looked to the clouds covering the moon and said, "Daddy, I've never been here at night. I can't get us across!"

His father picked Little Mo up and sat him on his hip till their faces almost touched.

"Son, the hour is at hand," he said. "You know that we call you Little Mo. But you know that is not your real name. Your name is Moses. Now, Moses, get us across that water!"

Moses leapt down and ran to the river. He dipped his arms into the chilly waters till he found the stone path. Quick as a bird, he flew across the stones and burst into Martha Tom's home.

"I'm sorry, I know it's late," he said. "But we are trying to cross the river. The men are after us, the men with the dogs and the lanterns and the guns. Can you help us?"

Martha Tom's mother jumped out of bed and talked as she dressed.

"Son, run to your family and hide them in the bushes near the path. Go, now, run! You'll know when to come across. Go! I have work to do!"

She went to every home in that village, pushed open the doors and called inside, "Women! Put on your white dresses! Bring a candle and meet me at the river. We're having a ceremony tonight, the crossing kind!"

And so it came to pass.

The guards stood on the slave side of the river with their dogs and lanterns and guns. Suddenly, they saw emerging from the white fog on the Choctaw side what looked to them like a band of angels. The angels carried candles that cast a halo glow in the fog around their faces.

Rising from the bushes and coming to life in front of them, the guards saw seven runaway slaves. They lifted their guns to fire.

They never shot their guns that night, for stepping out of the band of angels they saw the most beautiful little angel of them all. Her right hand held a candle, her left hand was outstretched, and she was walking on the water!

Martha Tom was singing a song she had learned at the slave church, but now she sang it in Choctaw.

"Nitak ishtayo pikmano
   Chissus ut minitit.
   Umala holitopama
   Chihot aya lashke!
   We are bound for the Promised Land!"

She took Little Mo by the hand, he took his mother, she took the children, they took their father, and together all seven of them went crossing Bok Chitto. When they reached the Choctaw side of the river, they blew the candles out and disappeared into the fog, never to be seen on the slave side again.

The descendants of those people still talk about that night. The Choctaws talk about the bravery of that little girl, Martha Tom. The black people talk about the faith of that little boy, Moses. But maybe the white people tell it best. They talk about the night their forefathers witnessed seven black spirits, walking on the water—to their freedom!

Chief Gregory Pyle
and Assistant
Chief Mike Bailey
lead hundreds of
Choctaws on a
Trail of Tears
Memorial Walk.

Choctaws Today: Two Prosperous Nations, One Strong People

FOLLOWING the signing of the Treaty of Dancing Rabbit Creek in September of 1830, the government forced thousands of Choctaws from their homes in Mississippi. The Choctaws began the trek to Indian Territory, thus becoming the first travelers on the Trail of Tears. Today the Choctaw Nation of Oklahoma numbers over 160,000, the third largest Native American population in the United States. Choctaw land stretches over a ten-and-a-half county area in southeastern Oklahoma, with the nation's capitol in Durant.

Choctaws who chose to remain in Mississippi were the forefathers of the current Mississippi Band of Choctaw Indians, now residing in and around Neshoba County. Tribal membership is over nine thousand, with 85% of Mississippi Choctaws speaking Choctaw as their first language and English as their second. While these Choctaws still weave baskets by hand from Mississippi swamp cane, they also weave wiring systems for the Ford Motor Company and the Chrysler Corporation, both with factories on tribal lands. Modern business and traditional culture live comfortably side-by-side.

While the Mississippi and Oklahoma Choctaws are similar in many regards—for instance, both are predominately Christian—one important historical distinction clearly separates the two nations. The narrative of the Mississippi Choctaws is a southern story, a remarkable story of refusing to leave home in spite of enormous pressures. The Oklahoma Choctaw story is one of tragedy and death on the Trail of Tears. However, in one common thread of narrative flow, in the celebration of the miracle of being, in the heroics of survival, both the Mississippi and Oklahoma Choctaws are seeds of a common thistle.

"We were kneaded out of this place."

—ESTELLINE TUBBY,
the most revered of
Mississippi Choctaw
storytellers

A Note on Choctaw Storytelling

Crossing Bok Chitto began as a song. In September of 1992, I made my first trip to visit the Mississippi Band of Choctaw Indians. Archie Mingo, a tribal elder, sang a song for me, the old Choctaw wedding chant. He was nestled in a caneback chair in the backyard of his home, facing the piney woods a few miles from Nainah Waiyah, the Choctaw Mother Mound. I later drove him to the mound and he stood on the crest of black earth, singing and recounting old stories.

On the return drive home, Mister Mingo pointed to a small home built of painted pine planks, now graying and warping with age. The structure sat a hundred yards or so from the road and was surrounded by oak and elm trees. Their branches hung thick with kudzu and red trumpet flowers.

"Those folks used to help runaway slaves," Mingo said, pointing to the now dilapidated Choctaw home.

I slowed my truck to a crawl and the trees seemed to part, allowing me a glimpse of a clearing where a wedding was taking place—a wedding from the past. Women in white linked arms and moved in an inner circle; men moved counter to the women in bright shirts and sashes, and the longing tone of the wedding chant smoked its way through yellowing autumn branches. Not far from the wedding clearing flowed the river Bok Chitto, where Choctaws once built stepping-stones to cross unseen, according to the storytellers, keepers of the history.

Louisiana Choctaws in full wedding attire, Bayou Lacomb, Louisiana, 1908.

Steeped in modern times of internet communication, with the razor edge of printed fact separating truth from untruth, it is difficult to imagine a world where the human voice reigns supreme. Yet, Native Americans live in a world that tends to accept the spoken word as the authority. Even today, many Choctaws are likely to trust a story told to them by another Choctaw more than anything they read on the printed page.

We Choctaws live by our stories.

Thus Martha Tom was born, and Little Mo, and the story *Crossing Bok Chitto*, a story about the spirit of freedom, a concept woven tightly within the fabric of this new country, this America we know and love. *Crossing Bok Chitto* is a tribute to the Choctaws—and Cherokees and Creeks and Chickasaws and Seminoles—and Indians of every nation who aided the runaway people of bondage.

Set in the old south, *Crossing Bok Chitto* is an Indian book, written by Indian voices and painted by an Indian artist. The story is documented the Indian way, told and retold and then passed on by uncles and grandmothers. *Crossing Bok Chitto*, in this new format—of language and painting, this book way of telling—is for both the Indian and the non-Indian. We Indians need to continue recounting our past and, from this book, non-Indians might realize the sweet and secret fire that drives the Indian heart. We are proud of who we are. We are determined that our way, shared by many of all races, a way of respect for others and the land we live on, will prevail.

We are people of the earth. Our faith and our stories are down to earth.
We are a working people who will never feel comfortable far from the earth.
When allowed our own plot of earth, we are at our best.

We will remain as close as possible to our rivers,
For they are intertwined with our faith.
We love the clean waters of our rivers.
We renew our strength by returning to our rivers.
We are baptized in our rivers.

We do not deny that darkness exists, but we chose to walk in light,
As a people, and for this choice we are rewarded with miracles in our lives.
To stay the darkness, we laugh at our frailties, and to stay the needs of others,
We reach out—and we give.
Our stories tell us this is the way it has been.
The telling of our stories assures us this is the way it will be.
You listen and you tell and you become.
As long as our stories are told,
We can be Choctaw forever.

Blessings to you all,
Tim Tingle

Visit us at www.cincopuntos.com or call 1-800-566-9072

Book and cover design by Vicki Trego Hill of El Paso, Texas. Printed in Hong Kong by Morris Printing.

FIRST EDITION 10 9 8 7 6 5 4 3 2
Library of Congress Cataloging-in-Publication Data. Tingle, Tim. Crossing Bok Chitto / by Tim Tingle ; with illustrations by Jeanne Rorex Bridges.   p. cm.   Summary: In the 1800s, a Choctaw girl becomes friends with a slave boy from a plantation across the great river, and when she learns that his family is in trouble, she helps them cross to freedom. ISBN: 978-1-933693-20-0 (paperback : alk. paper) 1. Choctaw Indians —Juvenile fiction. [1. Choctaw Indians—Fiction. 2. Slavery—Fiction. 3. Friendship—Fiction. 4. Indians of North America—Mississippi—Fiction. 5. Mississippi—History—19th century—Fiction.] I. Bridges, Jeanne Rorex, ill. II. Title. PZ7.T489Cro 2006 [Fic]—dc22 2005023612